anv

D1093977

HOCKEY CAMP
HUSTLE

BY JAKE MADDOX

text by
Melissa Brandt

STONE ARCH BOOKS
a capstone imprint

Jake Maddox is published by Stone Arch Books, an imprint of Capstone.
1710 Roe Crest Drive
North Mankato, Minnesota 56003
www.capstonepub.com

Library of Congress Cataloging-in-Publication Data is available on the Library of
Congress website.

ISBN: 978-1-4965-9699-4 (library hardcover)
ISBN: 978-1-4965-9915-5 (paperback)
ISBN: 978-1-4965-9750-2 (eBook PDF)

Summary: Zach is excited to be attending an elite hockey camp, but he quickly discovers
it's not all that he'd dreamed. He's feeling iced out by his older teammates, and one skater
seems to have it out for him. Will Zach and the other guys find a way to show some hustle,
work together, and take the camp tournament by storm?

Designer: Dina Her

Image Credits
Shutterstock: Brocreative, (grunge) design element, cluckva, design element, dotshock, cover
Eky Studio, (stripes) design element, Ronnie Chua, design element throughout

Printed and bound in the United States of America.
PA117

TABLE OF CONTENTS

CHAPTER I

A FAMILY GAME

When 14-year-old Zach Thompson stepped on the ice, he liked to list the names of his favorite professional hockey players.

T.J. Oshie, Devan Dubnyk, Mathew Dumba, Zach Parise, Mike Modano . . . , Zach thought as his breath formed a cold, gray cloud in front of his mask.

Although if Zach was being honest, T.J. Oshie was his absolute favorite. Both Zach and Oshie were from the same small town: Warroad, Minnesota, population 1,763.

Tonight's ice happened to be in the Thompson family's backyard. The yard wasn't big enough for a full sheet, but the family still had plenty of room to play. Also, if Zach's dad parked his car in the alley, the glow of the headlights let them skate into the night. Sometimes it was hard to see the puck when it crossed a shadow, but there was nothing better than playing in the dim light of winter.

"Zach! Heads-up hockey, buddy!" his dad yelled from across the ice.

Zach looked up just in time to see his sister Ashley charging toward him. She lowered her shoulder and drove him into the plywood boards that formed the edge of the rink. Zach stumbled backward, laughing.

"Hey," Zach said, pulling himself up, "this is a friendly game. No checking, dingus!"

"No name-calling!" Mom and Dad said at the same time.

Ashley smiled and crossed toward the goal, where Emma, Ashley's twin, squared up in the net.

For tonight's game, the family played half-sheet ice. It was girls against boys. It might have looked like an uneven matchup because the twins were younger. But when Ashley and Emma played together, it was like watching magic.

Zach's parents were no joke, either. His mom had played college hockey for the Wisconsin Badgers. She was the first African American goalie in the team's history. His dad had played wing for the University of North Dakota. Clearly, hockey was in Zach's blood.

Shaking his head, Zach pushed off the boards and raced toward Ashley. Her black curls bounced around the edges of her helmet as she skated down the rink.

Ashley passed to Mom, but Dad tipped the puck away. Zach scooped it up and took the puck back to center ice. Ashley hustled after him while Mom and Dad jostled for space in front of the net.

Zach backhanded the puck and slipped past his sister. He made a quick pass. Dad fired the puck toward Emma, but she easily blocked the shot.

The puck slid out in front of Zach. He nabbed it, made a tight turn in front of the net, and took another shot. Emma batted the puck away. Zach chased it to the corner and regained control before Mom could swoop in. A fierce hockey player, Zach was a blend of both his parents: dark hair, green eyes, and fast skates.

Zach pushed the puck back to the blue line and leaned in. He squared up for a power slap shot.

THWACK!

The puck buzzed through the air, pinged off the post, and popped into the net.

"G-O-A-L!" Zach yelled, pumping his fist.

"Wow, nice shot," Emma said as she got the puck.

Zach skated over and put his glove in front of her goalie mask. "Thanks, Em."

"Gross!" Emma said with a laugh. She pushed his hand away. "Your glove smells, doofus."

"No name-calling," Dad repeated.

"All right, team," Mom called. "It's time to head in. We have cake for the birthday boy."

"Cake!" Emma yelled and hurried off the ice.

The twins shoved their sticks into a plastic trash can at the side of the rink and went inside. With his legs wobbling and his hands frozen, Zach followed after. He stepped from the cold into the warmth of the kitchen and dropped down at the table.

Mom carried over a chocolate cake, the candles flickering bright. Zach's dad and sisters drew a breath. Together they started to sing, "Happy B—"

"Please, don't," Zach interrupted. "Please?" He could already feel his cheeks getting hot, despite the chill. Zach hated any kind of attention. The ice was one of the only places where he didn't feel shy.

"All right, birthday boy. No song. But you have to make a wish," Mom said, setting the cake down.

Zach smiled. He closed his eyes and blew out the candles.

"And we have a present," Dad said. As he started cutting the cake, Mom handed Zach a folded piece of paper with a ribbon around it.

"What's this?" Zach asked, shoving a forkful of cake into his mouth.

"Two summers of painting houses," his dad joked. Zach's dad was a teacher, and he painted houses in the summer to help bring in extra money.

Zach took off the ribbon and unfolded the paper. A faded brochure fell to the floor. Zach recognized it immediately. The brochure usually hung over his bed. It was for Camp Hapshire, an elite hockey camp. Zach had always wanted to go, but his family could never afford it.

"Read the letter," Mom said.

Zach felt his heart thudding as hard as if he were skating laps. "Welcome to Hapshire," he read aloud. He stared at the letter for a long second. Then he looked up at his parents. "I get to go? But . . . how? I never tried out."

"We sent them video highlights of your games. You leave next week, buddy," Dad said. "Unless you'd rather help me grade papers over winter break."

"Not only to camp. The *tournament* camp," Mom said, her brown eyes shining. "Better sharpen your skates!"

Zach went back to staring at the letter. He was still trying to process the news. "No way. Wow, thank you," he said. "I . . . really? For real?" Zach could feel a massive grin breaking across his face.

Mom laughed. "For real."

The twins jumped up and down. "Two weeks without Zach!" Ashley shouted.

"I'll miss you, too, dweebs," Zach said, but he couldn't stop smiling. Camp Hapshire's tournament championship game always made state news. A few of the players had even gone pro.

T.J. Oshie, Devan Dubnyk, Mathew Dumba, Zach Parise, Mike Modano, Zach thought. *And maybe, someday, Zach Thompson.*

CHAPTER 2

WELCOME TO HAPSHIRE

"Whoa," Zach whispered as he looked out the window of the Thompsons' family van.

The pictures in the brochure had not even come close to capturing the real Camp Hapshire. The camp was huge. It looked like a castle out of medieval times. A stone bridge with a big iron gate formed the camp entrance. Tall stone buildings covered the grounds. Each one had a triangle-shaped flag flowing above the roof.

Left of the entrance, two teams were already

battling on a pond-hockey rink. The pond made the Thompsons' backyard rink look like a puddle.

Zach's dad let out a long, slow whistle. He was impressed too.

Zach watched the skaters. They sped across the pond at a quick pace. Zach couldn't wait to get on that outdoor ice, but for some reason a pit was forming in his stomach.

After Dad parked, Ashley and Emma helped Mom lug Zach's equipment bag out of the van. Zach stepped onto the fresh snow and took it all in.

The camp hummed with activity. Other campers were hauling out their luggage and saying goodbye to their families. Coaches were shouting directions. Groups of guys were walking the winding paths between buildings.

There are so many people here, Zach thought. He felt his stomach tighten again. He shoved his hands into his coat pockets to hide the shaking.

Dad put a hand on Zach's shoulder. "It's okay to

be nervous, kid," he said quietly.

Zach nodded and let out a breath. Going to Hapshire was his dream. He couldn't let his nerves get the best of him. But Zach knew he had to get his family out of there. He didn't want to risk losing his courage and riding back home with them.

Zach grabbed his equipment bag from his sisters. He cleared his throat. "Well, looks like I better get inside," he said.

"So soon?" Mom asked, surprised.

"Sure thing," Dad said. He gave Zach's shoulder a squeeze. "Everybody in the car."

Mom wrapped Zach in a tight hug. "You'll do great. Before you know it, we'll be back, cheering you on in the tournament championship game!"

Zach watched as the van pulled away. Through the back window, he could see Ashley stick out her tongue and Emma press her face against the glass. Zach smiled and waved a final goodbye to his family.

It's now or never, he thought. He grabbed his gear

and followed other skaters into a huge stone building.

About a hundred or so kids buzzed around the drafty lobby of the campus center. Most of them looked older and bigger than Zach, and many stood together in clumps. It seemed as if everyone knew everybody else. Zach wondered if he was the only first-year skater.

As Zach stood alone, he tried not to gawk at the impressive facilities. From the glass lobby, he could see into every area of the building. There was a dryland practice area. There was an indoor pool. There were four ice rinks. There was a cafeteria. There was even a shop to buy smoothies. And every space was packed with skaters.

Zach suddenly felt more uncomfortable than ever. None of this was familiar. He thought of his quiet backyard rink. He imagined the peaceful *shush, shush* sounds his skates always made as he pushed the puck down ice at home.

What does the ice sound like here? Zach wondered.

Right now he could barely hear his own thoughts over the noisy crowd.

Then something bumped Zach from behind. A giant kid with a thick neck pushed past.

"Watch it," the kid said as he tromped to the opposite end of the lobby.

Nice, Zach thought. *My first run-in with another player, and he wants to punch me.*

Zach didn't have time to worry, though, as an older man with gray hair and a short beard stepped to the front of the room. He removed a silver whistle from his pocket and blew a sharp *chirp-chirp.*

"Listen up!" the man shouted. The room fell silent. "I'm Coach Holt. Welcome to Camp Hapshire. You're all going to be pushed hard over these next couple weeks. But if you're willing to dig deep and put in the work, you will be rewarded. I hope you're ready."

Zach tightened his grip on the strap of his bag. He hoped he was ready too.

"Now, everyone was assigned a team in their

acceptance letter," Coach continued. "Find your team's flag on the wall and gather with the other players. Let's move!"

Zach looked around the room for the Rockets and joined his team under the red banner. By the time he got there, the other boys were already standing in groups. Zach was just working up the courage to talk to the group next to him when the giant kid with the thick neck stomped over. He scowled at the other Rockets players.

"Don't embarrass me," he said, locking eyes with Zach.

Zach looked over his shoulder to see if someone was standing behind him. Nope, the kid was talking to him.

What's his deal? Zach wondered. He took a couple of steps to the side, separating himself from the giant kid and the rest of the team.

"You have an hour to grab some food before

drills," Coach Holt said. "No smoothies before then.
I don't want to have to clean strawberries off the ice."

Players dropped their bags into a pile and started
making their way toward the cafeteria, but Zach didn't
have much of an appetite. Instead he took his gear and
headed outside.

A sharp wind hit Zach as he stepped into the cold
daylight. The pond-hockey rink was now clear, and
Zach couldn't resist. An edge of snow made up the
sides of the rink. He set his bag down next to the snow
and put on his skates. He pulled out a helmet, gloves,
and stick too. Then he pushed onto the ice.

With each stride, Zach felt his nerves from the
morning calm. He practiced a quick-feet drill his dad
had taught him. Zach moved across the ice side to
side as fast as he could. Usually there were cones to
skate around, but Zach didn't need them. He knew
the distance from memory.

Zach practiced the drill over and over until sweat

dripped down his face. *This is why I'm here. This is why I wanted to come to Hapshire,* he thought. *To be a better skater.*

Zach lost track of time as he glided on the pond. When he finally looked up, the giant kid was standing at the side of the rink. His arms were crossed in front of his chest, and he was scowling again.

Zach made a sudden stop. It sent a spray of ice across the snow and in front of the other player.

"What's up?" Zach said. He was feeling braver after his skate. "I'm Zach Thompson."

"Yeah?" the kid said, still scowling. "I'm Ben, but I don't care what your name is. What are you doing out here? Trying to show off? Your legs are going to be Jell-O during drills. And if you ever spray me again, you'll regret it. Got it?"

Zach looked at his feet. "I was just—" he started.

"Yeah," Ben said, cutting him off. "Like I said, I don't care." Then he turned and walked away.

Zach leaned forward and tried to catch his breath.

It was only his first day at camp and he was already making enemies. He stepped off the ice and pulled at the laces of his skates. His mom had packed a clean towel in his bag, and he used it to wipe the sweat from his eyes.

Well, I know two things for certain, Zach thought, shaking his head. *That kid doesn't like me, and my legs really are Jell-O.*

It was too late to worry about it now. Flicking the snow off his blades, Zach shoved his skates into his bag and hustled toward the gym. Maybe a few of his other teammates were good guys.

CHAPTER 3

LINE DRILLS

Zach pushed through the Rockets' locker room door. A familiar mix of sweat, feet, and garlic hit his nose. He smiled. There was something special about the smell of hockey.

The room was crowded with guys. Most were talking and laughing as they pulled on their pads—except for Ben. Zach caught sight of the giant player off by himself in a corner. Ben glared. Zach quickly looked away.

Finding an open bench, Zach started getting ready. He couldn't help but notice that many of the other players had brand-new equipment. Their pads gleamed. Their sticks were top-of-the-line. It seemed as if Zach was the only one with gear that showed some wear.

"Gear is gear," Zach muttered. He pulled his dad's old UND socks over his shin pads and attached them to a strip of Velcro sewn under his breezers. Then he wrapped white tape around the top of his socks, just as he had done a hundred times before. The tape helped keep his socks from falling down on the ice. And the ritual always got Zach's head in the game.

After lots more tape, Zach tightened his skates. He breathed out. Now was his chance to show what he was made of.

The team shuffled from the locker room. Coach Holt stood next to the gate leading to the ice, handing out red jerseys. Zach got number four.

He pulled on the jersey and started skating and stretching his legs. Despite his time on the pond, they already felt solid again.

The Rockets were running drills with the Eagles team today. Holt stood on the players' bench and watched the skaters circle the ice. He blew his whistle to get the rink's attention. Zach and the others gathered in.

"You're all experienced hockey players, so we're not going to bother with easy stuff," Coach said. "Head to the red line. Do a V drill, full stop, then crossover and head back the other direction. Do five of those at my whistle."

Everyone got into position. Zach looked up and down the line of red and yellow players. He turned his feet at an angle, bent his knees, and waited for the whistle.

In that silent moment, Zach could feel himself smiling, despite his pounding heart. The shine and size of Hapshire might be strange, but the cold of the rink felt familiar. As shy as Zach was outside the rink, it all disappeared once he stepped onto a fresh sheet of glassy ice.

FWEEP!

The whistle blew. Zach leaned forward and raced up the ice, extending his legs with each stride. At the blue line, he skidded to a full stop, smoothly crossed one skate in front of the other to turn, and headed the other direction.

On his third pass, Zach's smile grew. He knew he was skating his fastest. From the corner of his eye, Zach could see someone on his heels, but he wasn't going to take the time to look. He focused on the ice in front of him.

At the last turn, Zach skidded to a stop and finally looked up. He was first. Ben skated in second, just behind him.

Ben glared at Zach as other skaters came across the line. When all the other players had finished, Coach shouted, "Let's see five more!"

FWEEP!

Zach dug in. After five sprints up and down the ice, he took first again. Ben came in a close second.

Zach could feel the other players studying him. Grateful that his cheeks were red from the drill and not embarrassment, Zach managed to nod at a couple of his new teammates.

"Grab your sticks and a puck!" Coach Holt yelled. Two captains started spreading mini orange pylons in four lines down the ice. "Speed skate through the cones while practicing stickhandling the puck. Form four lines, two on each end."

Zach lined up, first in his line. Ben skated over. He stopped in front of Zach and gave him a rough shove that nearly knocked Zach off his feet.

"Back up, Thompson," Ben said.

Zach scowled as he recovered his balance and took a step back. *Man, oh, man*, he thought. *This guy needs to get over it.*

The whistle blew and Ben powered off the start. The whistle blew again and Zach took off behind him, weaving through the cones. Without meaning to, Zach was soon closing the gap between Ben and himself.

He was about to slow when Ben glanced over his shoulder, then came to a sudden stop.

Zach had no time to react. He went full speed into Ben's back.

It was like running into a brick wall. Zach's equipment went flying. His gloves slid one direction and his stick slid another. Zach fell down hard onto the ice.

"Holy yard sale!" Ben said in a false voice. "Are you all right, newbie?"

A couple of the older players laughed. Zach's face burned as he grabbed his stick and gathered his gloves. His jaw went tight with anger. He expected this kind of play during a rough game. He had never been flattened in a practice before.

Zach's first hockey lesson at camp was not the one he'd expected: He needed to watch his back.

CHAPTER 4

ALL ABOUT DOUBT

The smell in the locker room before drill practice was nothing compared to the stench after. Zach and every other player dripped with sweat. One guy even threw up from pushing so hard. At least the kid did it in the locker room and not on the ice.

The smell wasn't what was bothering Zach most, though. Despite his sore legs, all he could think of was Ben's hit and the other guys' laughter. Camp was definitely not like skating at home. These guys were ruthless.

Ben had been on Zach's heels the entire practice. It was as if Ben had decided to make Zach look stupid.

It seemed to be working. When Zach plopped onto the bench, he felt the other players slide away from him.

As soon as Zach finished changing, he trudged alone through the chilly night toward the Rockets' dorms. Inside, he walked down a long hallway until he found the door with his name on it, along with two other names. Zach opened the door.

Two boys were already in the small room. One had long, blond hair and gave Zach a crooked grin. The dude looked like he belonged on a surfboard, not hockey skates.

The surfer held out his hand. "Hey. I'm Jackson, the Rockets captain."

Zach shook the other boy's hand. "Zach."

"Yeah, Yard Sale, right?" Jackson said, smiling.

Zach felt his chest go tight. He didn't smile back. *Great*, he thought. *Now my nickname is Yard Sale.*

"This is Sam," Jackson said, pointing to the other boy.

Sam was more serious-looking and shorter. He gave a silent nod.

Zach dropped his bag onto the open bunk bed and took out his cell phone. He tapped the screen and let his thumb hover over his "Dad" contact. He wanted nothing more than to tell his dad what had happened on the ice today.

But Zach tossed his phone onto the bed. *I can't do that to Mom and Dad,* he thought. *They worked hard so I could be here. I'm going to have to make the best of it.*

After an awkward moment of silence, Jackson spoke up. "It smells like pizza," he said.

Zach sniffed the air. It did smell like pizza. His stomach gurgled.

"I could eat an entire pizza," Jackson added. "Sam, go get us a pizza."

"Ugh," Sam replied, flopping onto his bed. "Get your own pizza, bro. My legs are still on the rink."

"What about you?" Jackson asked. He brushed his hair out of his eyes and stared at Zach. "Are you good?"

"Umm . . . ," Zach said, looking down. His throat suddenly felt tight. Thoughts started racing through his head. *What does Jackson mean? Is he talking about pizza . . . or camp? Does he think I need help on the ice dealing with Ben? Does he think I'm not good enough for the Rockets? For camp?*

"All right, good talk," Jackson said after several silent seconds. "I want pizza, so I'm out." He threw a peace sign up and left the room.

Sam looked at Zach, shrugged, and followed Jackson.

When the room was empty, Zach slumped onto the bed. His thoughts were still a mess. He had never felt quite so discouraged. Or exhausted. Or hungry. He didn't feel like being around anyone right now. Then his stomach growled again, refusing to be ignored.

With a sigh, Zach walked out the door.

In the common area, a dozen pizzas boxes were stacked on a table. A half dozen Rockets players were already eating.

As Zach grabbed a few slices, he thought he heard some of the guys snickering. Zach suddenly felt sure it was about him.

All the stress from the day seemed to wash over him. His cheeks burned. But it wasn't just because he was embarrassed. He was mad.

Zach stacked the slices, shoved a bottle of water into his pocket, and darted out of the common area. He wasn't about to hang out and become a joke. He ate the pizza and downed the water before he had even reached his room.

I'm not here to make friends, Zach thought as he slammed the door closed. *It doesn't matter if they like me or not. I'm here to skate.*

Zach threw his hockey bag off his bed, flopped onto the mattress, and closed his eyes. He fell asleep almost instantly.

* * *

When Zach opened his eyes the next morning, his roommates were already gone. *It's just as well,* he thought. He still didn't feel like talking anyway.

The frustration stayed with Zach as he pushed through the swinging door into the Rockets' locker room. A few players looked up and moved their equipment to take up more space on the bench. Jackson gave a smile, but Zach ignored him and sat on the opposite end.

Today was the Rockets' first game. It would count as part of the tournament. Zach just wanted to focus on hockey.

A moment later, Ben busted into the room. He stomped over and stood in front of Zach, waiting. Zach laced his skates and didn't look up.

"Hey, Yard Sale," Ben finally said.

"What?" Zach answered, keeping his eyes on his skates.

Ben bent down and said in a low voice, "Stay out of my way today."

Zach tied his other skate and pretended Ben wasn't getting to him. It was useless, though, because the pit in Zach's stomach had never felt bigger.

Only one week, five days, and three hours left of camp, Zach thought. *But who's counting?*

CHAPTER 5

RULES OF THE GAME

Zach stood alone next to the gate of the rink. He watched as the rest of the Rockets skated circles before the game.

You don't need them, he thought. *The ice is all that matters. Quick feet. Soft hands. Show them what you can do.*

After his personal pep talk, Zach stepped onto the ice. A mix of rock music pumped through the rink. Zach did his best to focus on his warm-up and not on how discouraged and angry he felt.

"Yard Sale! You finally made it," Ben shouted as he skated past Zach. A few of the other players snickered. "You might want to slow it down a little today," he added. "You never know what could happen during a game."

The Rockets captain glided toward them. "Knock it off, Ben," Jackson warned.

Ben shrugged. "Whatever," he said and sped away.

Zach didn't say anything as Jackson matched Zach's stride and skated next to him around the rink. Soon another player joined them as they moved to the back of the goalie net. He had braces and the smallest beginning of a mustache.

"Hey, Tyler," Jackson said. "Do you know Thompson? He was the wheels yesterday."

"Whoa, this is the kid who was on Ben's heels?" Tyler asked. He looked over at Zach. "Dude, it's like he hates you. Probably the only thing worse than playing against Ben is playing with him."

Zach stayed silent. He couldn't argue with that.

A whistle from Coach Holt brought the team to the bench. "Listen up! The play at Hapshire is different," Coach said. "Every one of our games is part of tournament play. So make it count today against the Eagles."

The coach started dividing the Rockets into four lines, or groups of players. Hockey game play was intense and tiring, so fresh players were subbed in frequently. Each forward line had a center and two wingers.

"Jackson, you're center on the first line," Coach began. "Zach, you looked good out there yesterday. Let's see what you've got as left wing today."

Zach couldn't help but smile. The first line was usually the team's strongest players.

Then Coach Holt continued, "Ben, let's try you on right wing."

Zach groaned. So much for good news.

After a sharp whistle from the referee, the first line of Eagles lined up against the first line of Rockets.

"I want to see good, clean play," the ref said.

Zach glanced over at Ben. *Yeah, right,* he thought.

At center, Jackson squared up against the opposing Eagles player. The ref blew the whistle and dropped the puck. It was time to see what the Rockets could do.

Jackson won the face-off and knocked the puck to Ben, who tossed it into the corner. Jackson hustled over and dug out the puck.

At the same time, Zach raced to the net to get in position for the pass. An Eagles defenseman was right on his tail, covering him.

Jackson looked out for Ben instead. But Ben wasn't in the slot, the area in front of the net. There was no one to take the pass.

The Eagles took advantage of the Rockets' disorder. They poked the puck away from Jackson and broke out of the zone.

The Eagles were fast. Zach, Ben, and Jackson had to hurry down the ice to get back in the play.

What was Ben doing? thought Zach as they rushed

over. *He might have scored if he had been where he was supposed to be!*

The Eagles quickly brought the puck down into the Rockets' side of the ice. The Rockets goalie dropped to his knees, getting ready to fight them off.

The Eagles wing made a sharp wrist shot. The puck bounced off the goalie's glove.

Zach picked up the puck before the Eagles could get it. He dished it to Jackson, who skated it outside the zone and passed to Ben. The right wing shot the puck down the ice, giving the Rockets time for a line change.

Zach, Ben, and Jackson hopped the boards to the bench. The second line raced out.

"What the heck?" Jackson said. He turned to Ben. "I was the first guy in, so you have to get in front of the net! Zach was covered."

"Seriously!" Zach added. "For all the chirping you're giving me, you'd think you'd at least be in the right position. It's hockey 101!"

"I think you should keep your thoughts to

yourself, newbie," Ben growled.

"Boys, that's enough!" Coach Holt said. "Tighten it up. A little more hustle and things will come together."

Zach shook his head. What was he doing? He never yelled at his teammates. *But I also haven't played on a team this disorganized since I was a PeeWee*, he thought.

Two more lines changed on the ice with no score. Then it was time for Zach's line to head back out.

The Rockets changed on the fly and were able to keep the puck in the opposing zone. Zach, Ben, and Jackson cycled the puck and moved it into the corner.

But as Zach tapped the puck toward Ben, the other wing fell out of position. He missed the pass. An Eagles player nabbed it and started racing down the ice.

Again! Zach thought as he hurried after the Eagles. *Does Ben want us to lose?*

Rushing into the play, Zach was determined to

make something happen. He swooped in and stole the puck from the Eagles center.

Zach passed to Jackson. The center took the puck and dodged a defenseman. He passed back to Zach, the puck spinning midair in a nice saucer pass.

Zach was ready. He snapped the puck in the upper corner and straight into the back of the net for a goal!

"Yes!" Zach yelled.

Jackson pumped his fist. "Nice!"

Ben slapped his stick on the ice in frustration.

Zach stared at the other wing. *What kind of guy doesn't celebrate when his team scores? At least I'm trying to get us the win.*

The line headed back to center ice for the face-off. The ref dropped the puck. Jackson won it again and passed to Zach.

Just as Zach was about to skate the puck into the Eagles' zone, something smashed into his side. He went sprawling across the slick ice.

Zach heard Ben laugh as he scooped up the puck.

He couldn't believe it. Ben had hip-checked him, his own teammate.

Ben sped toward the Eagles' goal, but it was no use. The Eagles defenseman darted in and poked the puck away. Zach scrambled to his feet and tried to get in the play, but the Eagles sent a long pass into the neutral zone.

The Eagles center moved the puck down the left side of the boards. He snapped a quick pass to the Eagles winger, who fired a shot. It flew between the goalie's legs. The game was tied.

Breathing hard, Zach and his line cleared the ice. The second line hopped out.

Ben dropped down onto the bench. "Way to go, Yard Sale," he said. "You should worry less about trying to be a superstar and more about staying on your feet."

"*What?* How was any of that my fault?" Zach shouted. He stood and stepped toward Ben. The older boy stood too. Zach kept after Ben, saying, "You checked your own teammate! Have you ever even heard the word *teamwork*? We'd be ahead instead of tied if you knew anything about hockey!"

"Hey! Enough!" Coach yelled, pushing the boys apart. "Get your heads in the game!"

Zach's head was buzzing as he sat down. He could hardly see. He had never felt so angry during a game before.

Out on the ice, the Rockets were doing no better. The team was breaking down. They were dropping passes. They were missing shots.

Soon, the Rockets defense couldn't hold the Eagles back any longer. Just before game time expired, the Eagles scored their second and winning goal.

CHAPTER 6

CAPTAIN'S PRACTICE

The Rockets silently filed into a classroom in the campus center. They had been equally quiet in the locker room after their embarrassing game. Everyone knew how poorly they had done. Coach had instructed them to clean up and then meet to break down the game play. Now here they were.

The players scattered themselves into the desks. Zach slumped into a seat closest to the windows, away from his teammates.

Coach Holt walked into the room, and Zach sat up straight.

The coach picked up a marker and went to the whiteboard. "What are the most important parts of a hockey game?" he asked.

The room stayed silent. Coach waited.

Finally, Jackson spoke up. "Skating," he said. Coach Holt wrote SKATING on the whiteboard.

"Shooting," Ben said.

"Puck control," added Sam.

Coach wrote both on the board. He looked at the list. "This camp is one of the most elite in the country," he said. "Each of you has all these skills. If they're all you need, you should have won the game today. Are you a great team?"

Zach stared at his hands. They were definitely not a great team.

"Then what's missing?" Coach Holt asked.

"Teamwork," Zach muttered, still looking at his hands.

"Say that again, Zach," Coach said, putting down the marker. "Louder, so everyone can hear, please."

Zach shoved his hands into the pockets of his joggers and turned bright red. He hadn't expected Coach to hear him at all.

"Teamwork," Zach repeated.

Coach Holt nodded. "You are all great skaters, great shooters, and great stickhandlers. Now you need to become great teammates," he said, studying each of the players. "Teamwork and heart are two of the most important parts of the game. You need to be loyal to your team and the game. If you aren't, you will not win."

Zach glanced at the other players. A few were nodding. Others looked at their shoes. Zach wondered if maybe he had been too quick to write them off. Sure, he had issues with Ben, but he hadn't exactly tried to make friends with anyone else.

"The games will only get harder," Coach continued. "You will have to support all of your teammates. If one fails, you all fail. The real work starts now. Any questions?"

No one said anything.

"Jackson, you're team captain. Lead by example," Coach Holt added. He looked out at the entire room. "Your next game is in three days. Learn to be a team."

The coach walked out, and the players sat in silence for a few moments. Then Jackson stood and came to the front of the room.

"I don't know about all of you," Jackson said, "but I'm here to learn from the best and to be the best. Our first game sucked. I don't want to go through that again, do you?"

Most of the players shook their heads.

"Everyone stand up and form a circle," Jackson said. "We're each going to say one positive thing about another teammate before we leave this room."

As the guys stood, Ben shoved his desk away. It made a sharp screech.

"You all can waste your time with this," Ben said. "But I've got better things to do, like actually practice." He stomped out of the room.

Zach watched the door slam shut. Maybe Ben wasn't willing to change, but Zach knew Coach was right. The team was missing heart. *He* was missing heart.

As Zach got into the circle with his teammates, he realized he barely knew any of their names. *I won't start caring about the Rockets until I get to know the other guys*, he thought. *I don't want to be here and be miserable.*

It was time to put himself out there. He cleared his throat and took a deep breath.

"Um, I don't even know everyone's name," Zach said, blushing as all eyes turned toward him. He looked at the ground. "Most of you guys know each other from past camps, right? How can I say something positive if I don't know you?"

Jackson stared at Zach for a moment. "Okay," the captain agreed. "Let's start by saying our names, where we're from, and why we play hockey."

Tyler stepped forward. "I'm Tyler from Minneapolis. I play because I like the attention," he said, smiling.

The other players laughed. Jackson grinned. "For real, Tyler?" he asked.

"Nah, I play hockey because I'm good and because it's exciting," Tyler replied.

One by one, each player gave his name and reason for playing. Zach agreed with most of what they said. The game was exciting and fun and he was good at it.

When it was his turn, Zach thought for a moment and said, "I'm Zach from Warroad. I play because my mom played and my dad played and his dad played. But mostly I play because I love the game. When I skate, that's all I'm thinking about. I don't worry about anything else. That is, until I got here. But I want to get that feeling back."

The entire team nodded in agreement, and Zach felt his shoulders relax a little. He hadn't even been aware they were tense.

"Hey, have you guys ever played shinny hockey?" Jackson asked.

Zach smiled. Shinny hockey was like regular hockey, except played indoors and on the players' knees. Zach had never met a player who didn't like it.

"Do you have a net?" Tyler asked.

Jackson shrugged and said, "I bet we can figure something out."

* * *

Before long, the entire team, minus Ben, found themselves back at the dorms. They had strapped on their shin pads, divided up into teams of three, and taken over the long hallways outside of the rooms.

Zach was on a team with Jackson and Sam. They were playing against Tyler and two guys named Carter and Alex. At first, Zach thought he would be too tired to be any good, but the soreness quickly disappeared as Jackson passed him the tennis ball. Zach slapped it back with the blade from an old wooden stick.

Jackson shot the ball toward Tyler, who kneeled in front of a mini plastic net. Tyler smacked it away.

Taking the rebound, Sam passed to Zach. Carter shuffled over and tried to get his stick around the ball, but Zach slid away. He came to the right side of the net. Tyler moved to block him, leaving the left open.

Zach saw his chance. He made a quick pass to Jackson, who shot the ball into the back of the net.

"Ugh, no!" Tyler said.

"Oh, man. Nice one," Carter added.

"We might actually win a game or two," Jackson said as he laughed and high-fived Sam and Zach.

Zach smiled. The hallway was crowded and loud. But for the first time at camp, he was having fun. Maybe these guys were okay after all.

"Yeah, maybe," Zach agreed.

CHAPTER 7

RED REIGN

Three days later, Zach sat down for lunch feeling exhausted. He and his teammates had been working harder than he'd ever worked at hockey in his life. They were waking up at six every morning, doing drills on the rink, running laps during breaks, and scrimmaging after lunch. Not to mention the dryland practice and discussing game-play strategy in the classroom.

No matter how tired they were, though, the team always made time to play shinny after supper.

Everyone except Ben. On the walk to the dorm, Zach usually spotted him practicing alone on the pond. Zach didn't mind that the older player hadn't joined the shinny games. At least after Coach's talk, Ben had stopped hounding Zach and had switched to simply ignoring him.

That was the camp routine now. Every night Zach dropped into bed and was asleep in an instant. It was tiring, but things finally felt like they were clicking into place.

Today, all Zach could think about was the upcoming game against the Blue Devils. After their loss to the Eagles, the Rockets had some catching up to do.

The Devils had won their first game in a 3–0 blowout. The whole camp was talking about it. There were still four games until the championship, but if the Rockets wanted a real shot at the first-place trophy, they had to impress. They had to beat the Devils tonight.

As Zach scooped pasta and garlic bread into his mouth, his teammates began to pile in around him with their lunch trays. Before he knew it, the table was full of tired Rockets players. Jackson had stepped it up as captain and encouraged the team to sit together. Most did, but Ben chose not to sit with them.

Between bites, the players talked hockey. Zach laughed as Jackson told a story about a time he had accidentally scored on his own team.

"It was literally my worst hockey moment ever," Jackson finished.

"Don't feel too bad," Zach said. "I think that's happened in the NHL a few times." Then he paused and added, "I mean, it's not something T.J. Oshie would ever do, but probably something a lesser player has done."

"Oh, man, Oshie is great!" Jackson said. "Did you see his shoot-out in the Olympics? Legendary."

Zach nodded. "He's my favorite player. Grew up in my hometown."

"No way! Really?" Tyler shouted. "Have you ever met him?"

"I wish," Zach said. "Who's your favorite?"

"Probably Dubnyk," Tyler said. "Because, duh, he's awesome."

"Mine's Sidney Crosby," Sam added.

"What? From the Pittsburgh Penguins? You gotta pick a Minnesota player," Tyler said. "Those are the rules."

"Whose rules?" Jackson laughed.

"Rockets' rules," Zach chimed in. "And red rules reign."

The entire table erupted in hoots and hollers. Jackson started chanting, "Red Reign, Red Reign, Red Reign!" Other players joined in, and soon Zach was stamping his feet and chanting too. The whole room was filled with the Rockets' shouts.

* * *

The energy from lunch carried over to the game that afternoon. Music blasted in the locker room, and the Rockets hit the ice in high spirits.

As Zach skated around the rink to warm his legs, he started listing his favorite players.

T.J. Oshie, Devan Dubnyk, Mathew Dumba, Zach Parise, Mike Modano . . . , he thought. A smile spread across his face. It was the first time he'd done that since leaving home.

The ref blew the whistle, and Zach moved into position at left wing on the starting line. Ben silently glided by into position on the right. Zach had almost forgotten he was there. He hadn't even seen him in the locker room.

As Jackson skated to center ice for the face-off against the Devils center, Zach's mind went back to the game. The Rockets were now better in sync off the ice. Zach hoped they were better on it too.

The referee dropped the puck. Jackson knocked it between both defensemen into the Devils' end. Zach crashed into the zone and fought a Devils defenseman for the puck in the corner. He wrapped the puck behind the net, and Jackson picked it up.

Jackson passed to Ben, who was in position in front of the net. Ben didn't hesitate. He fired a quick one to the upper-left corner.

Whump! The goalie caught the puck in his glove. The referee blew the whistle for a face-off deep in the Devils' zone.

The first line quickly skated off and hopped onto the bench. Zach was out of breath from his sprint into the zone. But somehow he felt even more energized.

"That was so close!" Zach said, flopping down.

"Yeah, nice shot, Ben. We'll get the next one," Jackson said.

Ben grunted but said nothing.

"Looking good, guys. Keep it up," Coach Holt said and rapped their helmets.

The second line kept up the pressure. They managed to keep the puck in the Devils' end for much of the play.

Unfortunately for the Rockets, the Devils goalie was on fire. He made save after save.

The third line rotated in on the fly. Alex was lined up to make a great shot when a Devils defenseman stuck out his stick and sent the Rocket tumbling to the ice. The Devils were called for tripping, and their player headed to the penalty box. The Rockets now had a five-on-four advantage.

Coach Holt sent out Zach's line early. "Here's our chance!" he said.

With a face-off deep in the Devils' zone, Zach moved into position, and Jackson squared up with the Devils center. Jackson won the puck and tapped it back to Sam on defense. It gave time for the three offensive players to spread out in the zone for the power play.

Sam passed it forward. Zach, Ben, and Jackson passed the puck back and forth, looking for their opening. The Devils tried to poke-check it away, but the Rockets kept the puck moving.

Jackson skated deep into the corner and passed out to the defense. Sam rifled a hard, low shot to the net.

Clang! The puck hit the pole and skidded back out.

Zach raced the Devils defense for the rebound, hustling from the corner to the net. He got to the puck first and fired a shot.

The puck bounced off the goalie's blocker pad. Zach caught the rebound again and immediately tipped the puck over the goalie's glove. It slid all the way back into the net. The Rockets had taken the lead!

The Rockets' bench erupted in cheers, and Zach threw his arms in the air. "*Whoooo!*" he yelled.

Jackson and Sam slid over and slapped Zach's helmet. "Great work, newbie!" Jackson shouted.

Smiling, Zach skated to the bench with the rest of the line. As he sat down, his teammates each gave him a quick high five.

Now this feels like hockey! Zach thought.

In the second period, the Devils were on the attack

and eager to score. The Rockets defense tried to hold them back, but the Devils slipped a shot in during a two-on-one rush. By the end of the period, the game was tied.

"Nice work, nice work," Coach Holt repeated as the team filed into the locker room during the intermission. "You're a different team than you were in the last game. Keep it up!"

Zach grabbed a water bottle and dropped onto a bench. Even though the game was tied, he was still smiling. Everyone seemed pumped. Tyler crashed in next to Zach, playfully shoving him over.

"Easy, dude," Zach laughed. As he took another gulp of water, he spotted Ben off by himself. Ben had his back to the room and was winding white tape around the blade of his stick. He seemed like he was in his own world.

"Calm down, guys," Jackson said, standing and raising his hands. "We still have another period to go. Red Reign!"

Chants of "Red Reign" followed the team as they stepped back out on the ice.

At the start of the third period, Jackson, Zach, and Ben hopped the boards to take on the Devils starting line. Jackson lost the face-off, and the opposing center shot the puck to the left side. The Devils winger took it and broke into the Rockets' zone. Zach and Ben had to back-check, skating fast to catch up to the play.

Meanwhile the Rockets defense got to work. They hounded the Devils and quickly recovered the puck. Sam passed to Ben, who shoveled it off the glass. Jackson picked up the puck in the neutral zone and passed to Zach.

Gliding into the Devils' end of the ice, Zach slowed the play at the blue line. He looked out for a pass. Both Jackson and Ben were covered, but Ben had the better angle on the net. As Zach looked back and forth between the players, he couldn't help but think, *Can I trust Ben? Will he make the right play for the team?*

Zach decided against Ben and drop-passed to Jackson. The center picked up the pace and quickly fired a slap shot. It bounced off the blocker of the Devils goalie.

Ben caught the rebound. Zach held his breath, waiting for Ben to take the shot. But the right wing hesitated. He dumped the puck into the corner instead.

What was Ben thinking? thought Zach. *He had an opening!*

Zach hustled to the corner and picked up the puck. Once again, he had to choose between passing to Jackson or Ben. But the doubt was still creeping around in Zach's head.

With a flick, Zach passed to Jackson. The center scooped up the puck and sent it back just as Zach sprinted to the front of the net.

The timing was perfect. The puck hit the tape on Zach's stick, and in the next instant Zach was tapping it in for the go-ahead goal. The Rockets were up, 2–1!

"Goal!" shouted Jackson.

As Zach high-fived his teammate, Ben skated toward the bench and slapped his stick against the boards. He had missed his chance to score. He and the entire team knew it.

The clock ran down, and the Devils scrambled to make something happen. But the Rockets kept the lead, winning the game by one goal. They were back in the race for the championship.

* * *

The locker room exploded with excitement after the game.

"Everyone meet in the dorm tonight!" Jackson shouted. "We're celebrating! Pizza, a video game tournament, and shinny hockey."

The team cheered, and Zach let out a loud hoot too. With a grueling week almost behind him and their first win on the board, Zach was ready for some fun. He high-fived Tyler, but then something caught his eye.

Ben had already jammed his equipment into his bag and was heading for the door. He left without saying a word.

As Zach watched, a twisting feeling gnawed at his stomach. The Rockets were playing better. They had pulled out the win tonight. But something still wasn't quite clicking.

CHAPTER 8

POND HOCKEY

Stepping from the rink into the night, Zach's nostrils burned from the cold and crisp winter air. The other Rockets walked toward the dorms. Zach pulled away from the group and went to the pond instead.

Ben was there, just as Zach expected. The older player was skating up and down the slick ice, practicing backward skating while stickhandling.

Man, that guy never quits, Zach thought. Ben was a rough skater, but while other players chilled and played video games, he was always out here. He was always pushing himself.

Tonight, Ben hadn't played the best, and it wasn't because he lacked the skills. The rift between the two Rockets wingers was holding Ben back. It was holding Zach back. It wasn't a fierce competition. It was bad teamwork, and they were lucky it hadn't cost them the game.

Zach knew if he truly wanted the team to succeed, it would mean including the *whole* team, even Ben.

"Hey, Ben," Zach called, his voice shaking a little.

Ben looked up and came to a stop. He stepped off the ice and came toe-to-toe with Zach. "What?"

"Why aren't you at the dorm?" Zach asked. "The team is celebrating."

Ben shrugged. "I'm not here to make friends."

Zach's shoulders slumped. That was exactly how he had felt at the beginning of camp. He had been so determined to focus on hockey, it had almost cost him the chance to know his team. It had also made him miserable. Maybe he and Ben were more alike than he thought.

In that moment, Zach did something he had yet to do at camp: he straightened and looked up. Sweat was soaking through the T-shirt underneath his hoodie. He was nervous, scared even. But he had to push through.

Zach locked eyes with Ben and said, "You're one of the fastest people I've ever skated against, but I don't trust you out there. The team doesn't trust you. You don't trust us either, and that's hurting all of us. We don't have to be friends, but it's like Coach said. We have to be able to support each other."

Ben squinted at Zach, not sure what to make of him. "Tell you what, Thompson, let's do five sprints on the pond. I win, and you never talk to me again."

"And if I win, you come back to the dorm. Celebrate with the team. Play shinny," Zach said.

"Whatever. I'm not worried about losing," Ben said, skating back onto the pond.

Zach laced up his skates, shoved on his helmet, and grabbed his mouth guard and gloves.

The two players lined up on the end of the pond. Zach dug in and bent his knees.

"Ready, get set, go!" Ben shouted, and the two took off down the ice.

Zach didn't waste time watching Ben's progress. He focused on stretching out his strides and using his full legs to push himself across the ice. Soon he had reached the other side.

He made a sharp stop, sending a spray of ice through the air. He did a fast crossover and raced back down the pond. By the time Zach was on his last turn, his legs were burning. He was pushing himself as hard as he could.

Zach used the edge of his blades to make his final stop. He looked up as Ben came in just a split second behind him. Zach had finished first. Ben knew it too.

Ben skated toward his bag, silent.

"Shinny," Zach said between panting breaths.

"Yeah, yeah," Ben muttered. Then after a moment, he added, "Who's playing, anyway?" He was still grumbling, but something in his tone had changed. Just a little bit.

Zach smiled. "Let's go," he replied.

* * *

Jackson and Tyler were already in the dorm hallway when Zach walked up with Ben. Their eyes widened. Zach could only imagine how surprised they were to see Ben and him getting along. *He* was still surprised.

Ben picked up a stick. He looked back and forth between Tyler and Jackson. They hadn't moved an inch. They were still just staring. "What?" Ben asked.

Jackson grinned and Tyler shrugged. Soon the other players had gathered and gotten into position. When they were all set, Zach faced off against Jackson with Ben as his winger.

Zach won the drop and passed to Ben, who immediately barreled down the hallway, knocking over players. Alex and Carter were two of the victims of Ben's shinny checking. Ben rushed the net and sent the ball sailing into it for the score.

"Ah, yeah!" Ben shouted, pumping his fist as Alex and Carter rubbed their sore elbows.

"Uh, Ben?" Zach said. "We play no-check shinny."

Ben looked around at the fallen players in the hallway. "Oh. My bad," he said. Zach thought he could see Ben's cheeks turn the slightest shade of pink. Ben tossed the tennis ball back to Zach. "I should've known you guys couldn't handle it. I'll save it for our next tournament game instead."

"Sounds like a good plan," Zach agreed, catching the ball.

Jackson and the others laughed as they got in position for another face-off. The Rockets' shouts and cheers echoed down the hallways as the game heated up, and they played until lights-out.

CHAPTER 9

THE CHAMPIONSHIP

Music shook the locker room as Zach laced up his skates for the last time at camp. Today was the day. It was Hapshire's championship game, the Rockets versus the Eagles.

The Rockets had fought hard for their place. They hadn't always been perfect during games, but every member of the team was now working together. Everyone was committed, and it had paid off.

Jackson sat next to Zach and taped up his stick. Ben sat a little farther down and adjusted his breezers.

"Did you see the news truck outside?" Jackson asked. His knees bounced up and down. It was the first time Zach had seen Jackson nervous.

Ben nodded. He looked a little frightened too.

"We've got this," Zach told them. "It's just like any other game."

Ben snorted. "Except it's televised, our families are here, and it's the championship game of one of the most elite hockey camps in the country."

"Well, yeah, other than that," Zach replied with a smile, "it's just like any other game." Ben and Jackson laughed as they all headed toward the rink together.

Zach's skates felt solid when he hit the ice. The news crew was filming the players during warm-ups. Zach grinned as Tyler stopped to pose for the camera.

T.J. Oshie, Devan Dubnyk, Mathew Dumba, Mike Modano, Zach Parise, T.J. Oshie, Devan Dubnyk . . .

The names rattled through Zach's head. His eyes scanned the crowd, searching for his family. The first thing he spotted was the red pom-pom of Ashley's

Wisconsin Badgers hat. The whole family waved, and Zach couldn't help but smile and wave back. He was still nervous, but he was also excited to show them how much he had grown during his time away.

The play clock ticked down the last few seconds of warm-ups. Jackson flagged everyone down.

"Huddle up!" the captain shouted.

The team formed a circle in front of the net.

"You guys know what we have to do. Quick feet. Play hard. Support each other. Red Reign on three," Jackson said. He put his gloved hand in the center, and the other players followed. "One, two . . ."

"Red Reign!" the team shouted.

While the others skated to the bench, Zach stayed out with Jackson and Ben for the face-off. Soon the referee glided in with the puck.

As Zach moved into position, he could hardly hear the crowd over his thumping heart. His breath was coming in and out of his body so fast, it was as if he had already played a period of hockey.

"Calm down, Thompson," he muttered to himself. *Just another game, right?* he thought as his hands dripped sweat inside his gloves. *This is what you're here to do. To play great hockey with a great team. A real team.*

The sound of a whistle brought Zach back to the game.

"Red, you all set?" the ref asked. Jackson nodded. "Yellow?" The ref looked at the Eagles front man. The center nodded.

The ref got a wave from both goalies. Then he blew the whistle and dropped the puck.

The Eagles center won the face-off and dumped the puck in the Rockets' end. Tyler was on top of it before the Eagles offense could make a move. He made a wide loop and shoveled the puck to Ben.

Ben snapped a pass to Zach, but an Eagles player darted in before Zach could get his stick on it. The opposing player took the puck and raced toward the net. He quickly fired a shot. The puck bounced off the goalie's glove.

The Eagles center was waiting for the rebound. He easily tapped the puck into the net.

Zach was stunned. It was less than thirty seconds into the game, and the Rockets were down 1–0.

Coach Holt signaled for a line change. The second line for the Rockets jumped over the boards as Zach, Jackson, and Ben hopped to the benches. The three leaned against the edge of the board, breathless as they watched the second line play.

"What. Was. That?" Ben asked no one in particular.

"That was not good," Zach agreed, and the words were no sooner out of his mouth than the Eagles sent the puck flying into the Rockets' net again.

"No!" Jackson yelled.

"You've got to be kidding!" Ben shouted, slapping the boards.

Zach looked up at the play clock. Only two minutes had passed, and the Rockets were down 2–0. He looked down the bench at his teammates and felt more determined than ever. He wasn't going to let them or himself feel defeated. "We knew this game would be tough. We're not giving up."

Jackson and Ben nodded, trying to ignore the cheers of the Eagles' celebration out on the ice.

The Rockets third line came out strong. They managed to hold the Eagles to a two-goal lead. Play stopped after the puck flew over the glass.

Zach and the rest of his line hopped the boards, ready to go back on the ice.

"We've got work to do, guys," Coach hollered. "Protect the puck and get it out of our zone."

The whistle blew and Jackson won the puck in the face-off, passing to Ben. Ben looked across ice at Zach, but Zach couldn't lose the defenders who crowded him. Ben snapped the puck back out to Sam on defense. Except Ben overshot it. The puck zipped past Sam and off the boards, straight to an Eagles player.

Ben yelled, frustrated, and smacked his stick on the ice as the Eagles took the puck toward the Rockets' zone.

"Stay focused!" Zach shouted to Ben.

Bolting down the ice, Zach barged into the action. He was able to intercept a pass and steal the puck. Zach took it back into the Eagles' end of the ice.

As the first period wound down, the Rockets kept the Eagles out of their zone. But the offensive line wasn't clicking. The Rockets couldn't manage to put up any points, and the period ended with the score remaining 2–0.

The team shuffled into the locker room to regroup after the first period meltdown. Zach dropped onto the bench next to Jackson as he removed his helmet. He wiped the drips of sweat from his forehead.

"That was rough," Coach Holt started. "But great teams know how to come from behind." He looked around the room. "Do you have the heart and teamwork to make it happen?"

"Yes, Coach!" Zach and the others shouted.

"Then go out there and show them!" Coach Holt added with a sharp clap.

As cheers broke out in the locker room, Zach moved down the bench to where Ben was sitting alone. Zach knew if he had messed up, he would be kicking himself over it.

"Hey, don't sweat it, man. There's lots of time left," Zach said.

Ben stared at his gloves. Then he looked up and grinned. "Relax, Yard Sale. It's just another game."

"You know, that name is starting to grow on me," Zach said with a laugh, holding up his fist.

Ben bumped it as they walked with the rest of the team back out to the rink, cheers of "Red Reign" following behind.

CHAPTER 10

BOTTLE ROCKET

The mood felt different as the Rockets took to the ice for the second period. Zach exchanged a nod with Jackson and Ben as they got into place for the face-off. They were ready to fight.

The puck dropped for the face-off, and the Eagles nabbed it just like they had first period. But this time the Rockets defense sprang into action. They quickly recovered the puck. The defensemen passed to Zach, and he hustled down the ice, his heart pumping.

After two quick passes from Zach to Jackson and back, the Rockets brought the puck into the Eagles' end. The Eagles line had to race to catch up to the play.

As the Eagles scrambled, Jackson passed to Zach, who was deep in the Eagles' corner. At the same time, Ben raced to the opposite corner. Zach could see Jackson jostling for space near the net, so he passed the puck behind the net and around the boards to Ben.

Zach darted to the front of the net, near the crease. With a quick flick, Ben passed back to Zach, who immediately shot the puck.

The goalie shifted left to block the shot with his leg pad. The puck bounced out, but Zach caught the rebound. He tipped the puck, and it slid right under the goalie's blocker for a goal.

"*Whooo!*" Zach yelled as Jackson and Ben rushed over to him.

"Nice shot, man," Ben said, slapping Zach's helmet.

"Thanks for the pass," Zach replied. "See? We've

got this!"

"Well done!" Coach Holt shouted when Zach and the others skated in for the line switch.

The Rockets second line did just as well. The center hustled for a two-on-one as he sped toward the Eagles' net. He blasted a shot quickly from the slot.

The goalie didn't have a chance to prepare. The puck flew in for the tying goal.

From the players' bench, Zach and his teammates leaped to their feet. "Yes!" Zach cheered. "Sweet goal!" The Rockets were really in it now.

Time seemed to fly off the clock. The second period went by with both teams fighting to take the lead. The Rockets were pushing hard on offense, but the Eagles battled the puck out of their zone and kept the Rockets defense busy. No one was able to edge ahead, even as the third period started and ticked down.

Now twenty seconds remained on the clock. The game was still tied.

The Rockets first line hopped the boards. Zach

knew this was their last chance to make something happen.

All thoughts of the TV cameras, the sea of spectators, and even his own family disappeared from Zach's mind. He let out a deep breath as he glided across the ice. Just like at home, he was only thinking about hockey.

Jackson passed to Zach from the left side face-off dot in the Eagles' zone. Zach skated the puck out to center ice, looking for his teammates. Both Ben and Jackson were elbowing for space in front of the net.

This is it, Zach thought. He briefly locked eyes with Ben before focusing back on the goalie.

Zach started to wind up for a slap shot. The Eagles goalie dropped to his knees for the block.

But as Zach brought his stick down, he angled the hit to the right. The puck flew to Ben, who flicked it toward the top of the net.

The puck went hurtling in so fast it popped the

goalie's water bottle off the net and onto the ice.

Goal! The game buzzer sounded. The Rockets had taken the win, and the tournament, 3–2!

Zach raced over to Ben. "Killer bottle rocket, man!" he shouted.

"That fake wasn't too bad either!" Ben replied, slapping Zach's shoulder as all the Rockets players flooded the ice and surrounded them both in celebration. Zach yelled and cheered with the rest of his team.

* * *

After the big win, the Rockets went wild in the locker room. No one was in a hurry to head out. Zach, Ben, and Jackson kept breaking the game down, giving play-by-plays for each moment that led to the team's victory. Zach's cheeks hurt from smiling so much.

"It was like I could read Yard Sale's mind,"

Ben was saying. "When he was winding up, I just knew—"

Just then, Coach Holt approached Zach. "Thompson," he said.

Ben and the entire room quieted. "Yes, Coach?" Zach asked.

"Nice job today," Coach Holt said and flipped him the game puck.

Zach caught it and stared at the black, roughed-up surface. "Thanks, Coach," he whispered. He couldn't believe he'd almost quit at the beginning of camp. Now here he was, two weeks later, a champion who wasn't yet ready to leave camp—or his team.

Zach stared at the puck a moment longer. Then he turned and passed it to Ben.

"You're the hardest-working player I know," Zach said.

Ben's mouth dropped open as he took the puck. "Whoa. I mean, thanks, Zach."

Zach grinned. "What, no Yard Sale?"

"Nope, not anymore," Ben replied.

"So . . . ," Zach said, looking around at his teammates. "Anyone up for one final game of shinny?"

The room erupted in cheers, the players scrambling to their feet.

ABOUT the AUTHOR

Melissa Brandt has written a number of short stories, children's books, and feature-length screenplays. She was awarded the 2012 McKnight Fellowship for her screenplay called *Chicken Day*. She grew up in Worthington, Minnesota, and now lives in Rochester, Minnesota, with her hockey-playing, hockey-loving family.

GLOSSARY

drill (DRIL)—an exercise in which you do the same thing many times in order to learn a specific skill

elite (ih-LEET)—the best or most skilled at something

embarrass (em-BAIR-uhss)—to make someone feel foolish, especially in front of others

exhausted (ig-ZAW-sted)—very tired and completely worn out

glide (GLAHYD)—to move in a smooth way

hustle (HUH-suhl)—to act quickly and with energy

rebound (REE-bound)—a puck that bounces back after hitting something

reign (RAYN)—the period in which a group is the best

support (suh-PORT)—to help and encourage others

wing (WING)—a position in hockey in which the player plays mostly on either the left or right side of the rink; also called a winger

zone (ZOHN)—one of three areas on a hockey rink marked by two blue lines

DISCUSSION QUESTIONS

1. In your own words, describe how Zach feels during the first few days at camp. Point to examples from the story to back up your answer.

2. After the game against the Blue Devils, Zach talks to Ben on the pond rink and invites him to celebrate with the team. Why does Zach decide to do this? Do you agree with his choice? Why or why not?

3. The Rockets had to work together as a team to succeed on the ice. Talk about a time when you worked with others to do something. How did it go? What was difficult about being in a group? How was it helpful?

WRITING PROMPTS

1. Do you think Zach's time at Camp Hapshire was valuable? Why or why not? Write three paragraphs arguing for your answer, and be sure to use examples.

2. This story is focused on Zach. It shows his feelings and reactions to situations. Imagine if the story was focused on a different character. Choose a moment in the book and rewrite it from Jackson's or Ben's point of view.

3. Have you ever attended a camp for a sport or other activity? Write about your experience. Would you recommend it to others? If you haven't been to camp, write about the kind you would like to go to and why it would be useful.

HOCKEY LINGO

Hockey is a fast-paced and physical game. Lots of creative slang for the action and gear has found its way into the sport. Become a pro fan and get to know some of the most colorful terms!

biscuit—another word for the puck

bottle rocket—a goal that hits the net so hard it knocks the goalie's water bottle off the top of the net

bucket—a hockey helmet

butterfly—a position in which the goalie has his/her knees and arms spread wide

cherry-picking—waiting for an easy goal or easy play

chiclets—a hockey player's teeth

chirping—yelling at or harassing other players or the referee

duster—a player who spends a lot of time on the bench and doesn't play much

face wash—when a player puts his/her smelly glove in the face of another player

flow—the long hair a hockey player has that sticks out from underneath the helmet

go-ahead goal—the goal that puts a team one point ahead of the opposing team

hat trick—when a player gets three goals in one game

hot hands—a player who is getting a lot of goals or assists

pipe—the goal post

saucer—a puck that floats through the air when passed

sin-bin—the penalty box

wheels—a fast or skilled player

where mama keeps the peanut butter—a goal that is scored at the top of the net or on the "top shelf"

yard sale—when a skater trips or falls and his/her equipment scatters across the ice, similar to items at a garage or yard sale

FOR MORE
ACTION ON THE ICE RINK,
PICK UP . . .

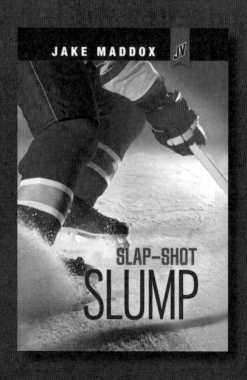